And if I have prophetic powers,

and understand all mysteries and all knowledge,

and if I have all faith, so as to move mountains,

but have not love, I am nothing.

◆

—I CORINTHIANS 13:2

REVISED STANDARD VERSION OF THE BIBLE

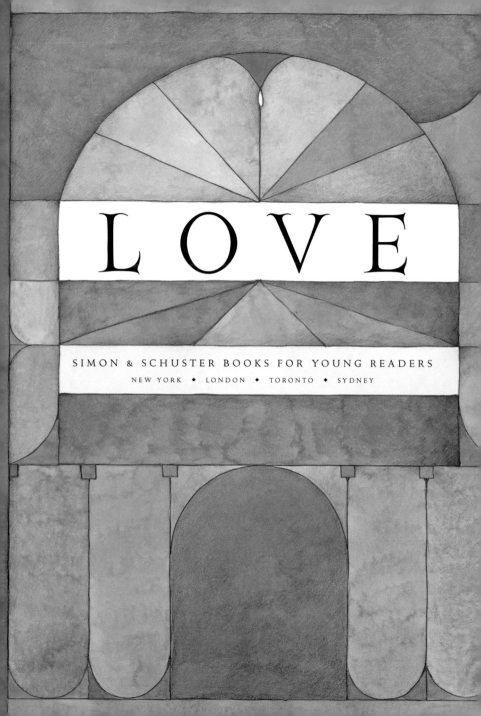

LOVE

SIMON & SCHUSTER BOOKS FOR YOUNG READERS

NEW YORK • LONDON • TORONTO • SYDNEY

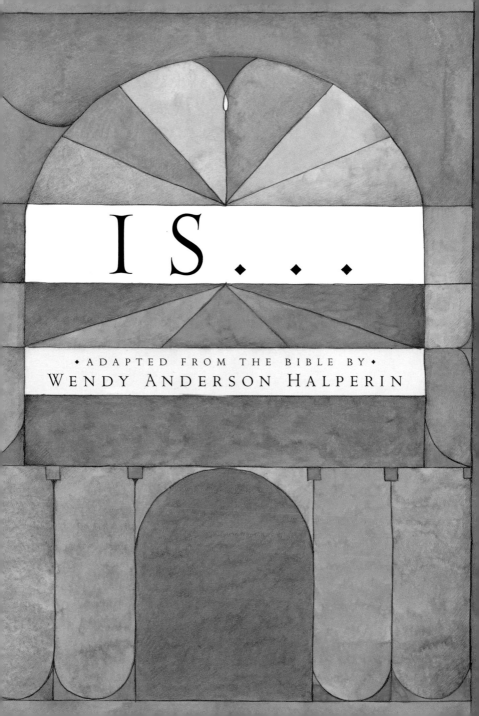

I S . . .

• ADAPTED FROM THE BIBLE BY •

WENDY ANDERSON HALPERIN

OVE . . .

IS PATIENT. LOVE IS KIND.

L OVE . . .

IS NOT ENVIOUS OR BOASTFUL.

OVE . . .

IS NOT ARROGANT OR RUDE.

OVE . . .

DOES NOT INSIST ON ITS OWN WAY.

OVE . . .

IS NOT IRRITABLE OR RESENTFUL.

OVE DOES NOT REJOICE IN WRONGDOING,

BUT REJOICES IN THE TRUTH.

OVE . . .

BEARS ALL THINGS.

OVE...

BELIEVES ALL THINGS.

OVE . . .

HOPES ALL THINGS.

L OVE . . .

ENDURES ALL THINGS.

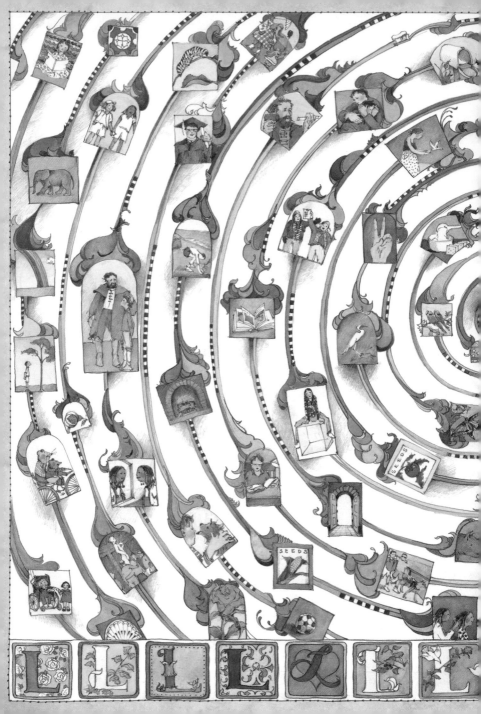

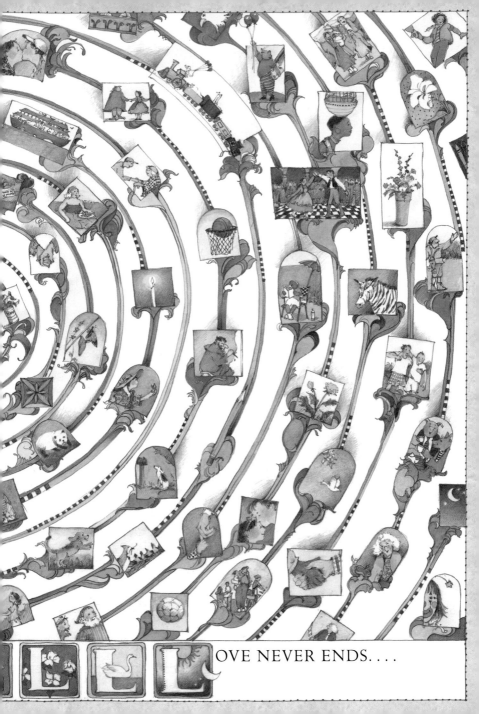

OVE NEVER ENDS. . . .

◆ A Note from the Illustrator ◆

To create the illustrations in this book
I used pencil and watercolors. The ideas for the
numerous scenes depicted on each spread came not only
from me, but also from my children, our friends, and our
relatives. I loved illustrating these words, and if there's
one thing I've learned from the experience, it is that how
we respond to any person, any object, any situation is our
choice. We can choose to approach these things with
envy or arrogance, impatience or selfishness . . .

. . . or we can choose to act with love.

Simon & Schuster Books for Young Readers

An imprint of Simon & Schuster Children's Publishing Division

1230 Avenue of the Americas, New York, New York 10020

Copyright © 2001 by Wendy Anderson Halperin

All rights reserved, including the right of reproduction in whole or in part in any form.

SIMON & SCHUSTER BOOKS FOR YOUNG READERS is a trademark of Simon & Schuster, Inc.

Book design by Heather Wood with Wendy Anderson Halperin

The text for this book is set in Golden Cockerel and Cochin.

The illustrations are rendered in watercolor with pencil.

Manufactured in China

First mini edition, 2006

2   4   6   8   10   9   7   5   3   1

CIP data for this book is available from the Library of Congress

ISBN-13: 978-0-689-87618-9

ISBN-10: 0-689-87618-1

first edition

◆ A Note on the Text ◆

What is love?
The apostle Paul attempted to define the word
for the followers of Christ living in the Greek city of Corinth in 56 A.D.
Almost two thousand years later, one part of his definition has come to exemplify
ideal love for countless people the world over. Often referred to as "The Way of
Love," Paul's words in I Corinthians 13 have been translated (and retranslated)
from Greek into a host of different languages. But no matter how many times
these words are translated, their essential message — that the love we express
is best defined by our attitudes and actions — remains constant.

For this abridged version of "The Way of Love," several English translations
of the Bible have been consulted. They include the King James Version,
the Holy Bible, New International Version,
and the Revised Standard Version.

And now these three remain:

faith, hope, and love.

But the greatest of these is love.

◆

—I Corinthians 13:13

Holy Bible, New International Version